THE TOOTH FAIRY

VS.

THE EASTER BUNNY

FOR MY SON ALEXANDER, WHO ENCOURAGED ME TO WRITE
THIS STORY, AND HIS TOOTH FAIRY, GREEN, WHO BRINGS
MAGIC AND JOY TO OUR LIVES—JLBD

TO MY SISTER MELANIE AND NIECE GIGI,
WHO BOTH ENJOY THE EASTER BUNNY'S VISIT
(AND HIS CHOCOLATE EGGS) EACH YEAR!—EH

PENGUIN WORKSHOP
An Imprint of Penguin Random House LLC, New York

Penguin supports copyright. Copyright fuels creativity, encourages diverse voices, promotes free speech, and creates a vibrant culture. Thank you for buying an authorized edition of this book and for complying with copyright laws by not reproducing, scanning, or distributing any part of it in any form without permission. You are supporting writers and allowing Penguin to continue to publish books for every reader.

Text copyright © 2020 by Jamie L. B. Deenihan. Illustrations copyright © 2020 by Erin Hunting.
All rights reserved. Published by Penguin Workshop, an imprint of Penguin Random House LLC, New York.
PENGUIN and PENGUIN WORKSHOP are trademarks of Penguin Books Ltd, and the W colophon is a registered trademark of Penguin Random House LLC.
Manufactured in China.

Visit us online at penguinrandomhouse.com.

Library of Congress Cataloging-in-Publication Data is available upon request.

ISBN 9780593094051   10 9 8 7 6 5 4 3 2 1

THE TOOTH FAIRY

VS.

THE EASTER BUNNY

BY JAMIE L. B. DEENIHAN
ILLUSTRATED BY ERIN HUNTING

PENGUIN WORKSHOP

Blue had always dreamed of earning a spot on the Tooth Fairy Team, and after years of hard work, his dream came true.

On his days off, Blue finally had time for other things besides studying and training.

He relaxed at the Flitter Flutter Spa,

wrote to his pen pal,

and visited with friends in the rescue department.

Blue didn't think life could get any better, until Luna, captain of the Rescue Squad, revealed one of her new inventions.

"What is that?" asked Blue.

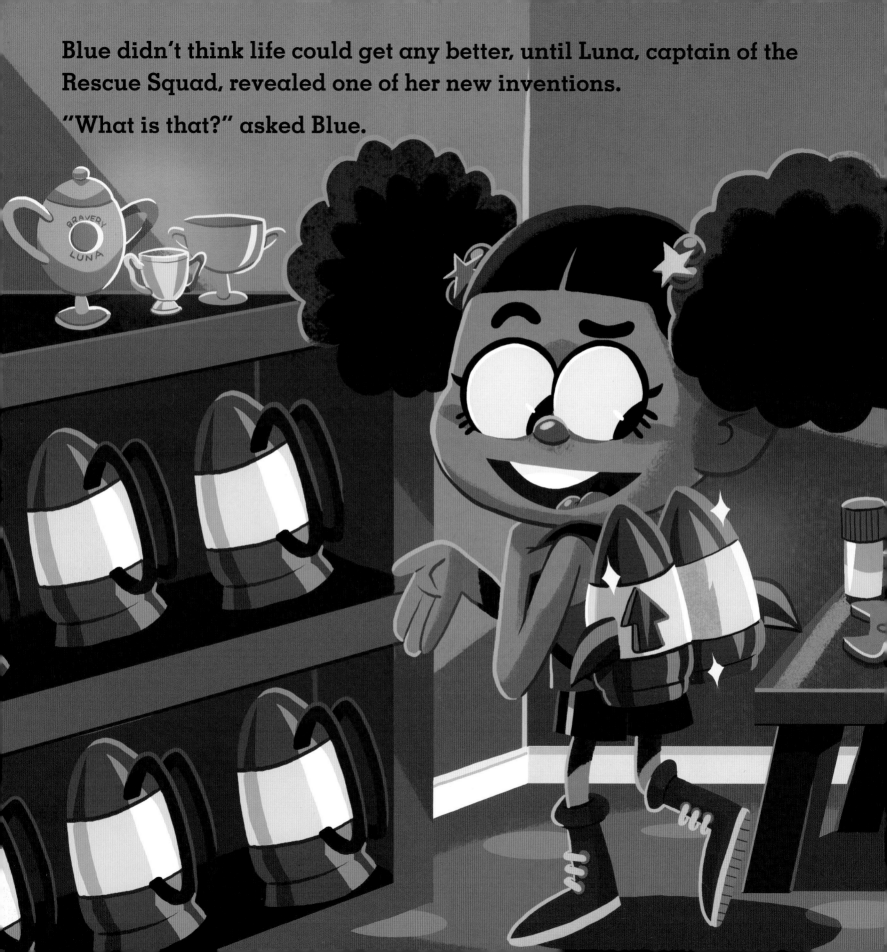

"It's the Rescue Squad Super-Speed Jet Pack 2.0," announced Luna.

"What does that button do?" Blue asked.

"Let me show you!" said Luna.

Luna was preparing for her first test flight around Toothtopia with the new jet pack when, all of a sudden, Blue's Lost Tooth Indicator buzzed.

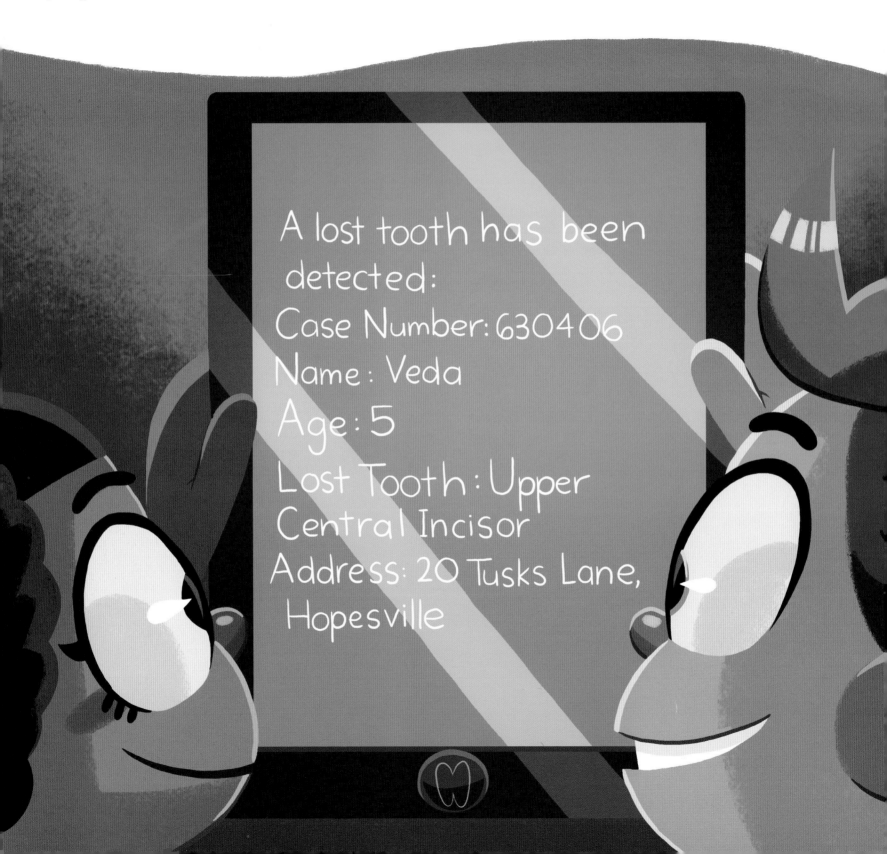

A lost tooth has been detected:
Case Number: 630406
Name: Veda
Age: 5
Lost Tooth: Upper Central Incisor
Address: 20 Tusks Lane, Hopesville

"Will you show me how the jet pack works when I get back?" asked Blue.

"Absolutely!" said Luna. "And don't forget to call for backup if you run into any problems."

But Blue wasn't worried. What could go wrong?

He entered Veda's address into his Tooth Locator Device and was off!

Blue's flight went smoothly,

and he used his pixie-dust pen to get into Veda's house.

Once inside, Blue spotted something interesting.

"Why would Veda leave me a basket of colorful eggs?" he wondered.

Blue was checking his Tooth Fairy Handbook for an explanation when he heard someone hop into the room.

"Step away from the basket," a voice warned.

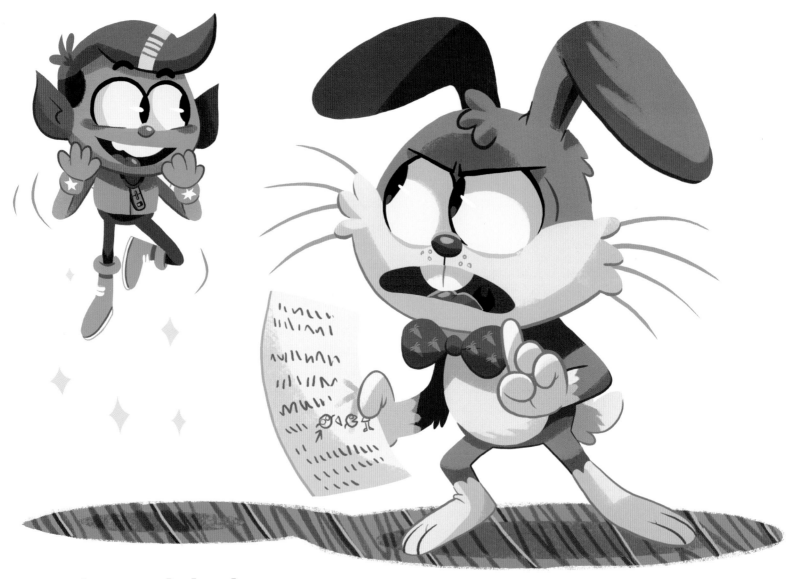

Blue turned around slowly.

He saw floppy ears, a fluffy coat, and a perfect set of upper central incisors.

"You must be Veda's pet bunny!" said Blue. "Aren't you just the fluffiest little—"

"Hands off the fluff, Blue," snarled the bunny.

Blue was surprised. "Who are you? And how do you know my name?"

"I'm the Easter Bunny, and I know your name because Veda left us this note. And look—she put *your* name first."

Dear Blue and the Easter Bunny,

I've been doing everything I could to lose my wiggly tooth the night before Easter, and look, it worked!

Will you please hide the Easter eggs together this year? Blue, maybe you could hide my Tooth Fairy coin in an Easter egg instead of putting it under my pillow?

Love,
Veda

Me →

wiggle wiggle!

crunch crunch

me again!!

yum yum

PS-The kids at school have been teasing my little brother, Frankie, because he believes in the Easter Bunny. He wants to trap the Easter Bunny to prove he's real, but I told him that's not a good idea.

Can you help him?

"Wow! You really *are* the Easter Bunny! It would be an honor to hide eggs with you!" said Blue. "I've had lots of practice hiding coins under pillows, so I'm sure I could—"

The Easter Bunny cut Blue off. "Only the Easter Bunny hides Easter eggs."

Blue tried to explain, "But I can help. We'll—"

The Easter Bunny hopped closer,

and closer,

and closer,

until his whiskers tickled Blue's cheek.

"I work alone, Blue. Always have, always will. You can't teach an old bunny new tricks."

"Then I propose a challenge!" declared Blue.

Blue switched his pixie-dust pen to the chalk setting to create a scoreboard.

"If you win, I'll leave, so you can work alone tonight," Blue explained.

The Easter Bunny liked that idea.

"But if I win, we hide your eggs and Veda's Tooth Fairy coin together," Blue added.

"Deal," said the Easter Bunny.

They shook hand and paw, and the competition began.

The Easter Bunny jumped higher,

aimed more accurately,

and balanced better than Blue.

"You win, Easter Bunny. I'll head back to Toothtopia right away."

"Safe travels, Blue."

With Blue out of his way, the Easter Bunny thought he'd grab a quick snack before hiding the eggs.

But something went terribly wrong.

"It's a trap!" wailed the Easter Bunny.

Blue was outside and already on his way home when he heard the Easter Bunny yelling.

"Easter Bunny!" exclaimed Blue.

Blue tried to untie the ropes, but it was too difficult. "Is there someone from your company you can call for help?"

"I told you, Blue. I work alone," said the Easter Bunny.

"What about your family?" asked Blue.

The Easter Bunny tried to hide his tears. "It's just me, kid."

"I'm going to help you," promised Blue.

"A little Tooth Fairy like you could never get me out of this mess," said the Easter Bunny.

"Maybe I can't," Blue replied, setting his pixie-dust pen to the walkie-talkie setting. "But I don't work alone."

Blue made a call to the T. F. Command Center, and within minutes, a fleet of fairies arrived on the scene.

"Easter Bunny, meet Luna! She's the leader of the Rescue Squad," announced Blue.

"At your service," said Luna. "We'll have you out in no time!"

"Thanks for helping me," said the Easter Bunny. "I'm not sure how I can ever repay you."

"How about letting us help you hide these Easter eggs?" suggested Blue.

The Easter Bunny liked that idea.

Together, they hid Easter eggs,

wrote back to Veda,

and used the camera setting on Blue's pixie-dust pen to create a very special Easter gift for Frankie.

Dear Veda,
Congratulations on losing your second tooth the night before Easter! We worked together to make this the best Easter-egg hunt ever! We hid your Tooth Fairy coin in one of the eggs. Happy hunting!
Love,
Blue and the Easter Bunny
P.S. Please give this photo to Frankie. It should help him with the kids at school.

Blue, Luna, and the Rescue Squad fairies gave the Easter Bunny a hug goodbye.

"Thank you, everyone," said the Easter Bunny. "You all make such a great team."

Blue checked the T. F. Handbook. "You know, there aren't any rules about bunnies coming to Toothtopia. If you like working with a team, you're welcome to join ours."

"But how would I get there?" asked the Easter Bunny.

"I have an idea . . . ," said Luna.

Everyone at the T. F. Command Center was excited to meet the Easter Bunny.

They even taught the old bunny some new tricks.

Until Veda lost another tooth the night before St. Patrick's Day.

But Blue wasn't worried. What could go wrong?